NICKELODEON®

The WILD Thornberrys™

In Too Deep

by Kitty Richards

illustrated by the Thompson Bros.

Ready-to-Read

Simon Spotlight/Nickelodeon

New York   London   Toronto   Sydney   Singapore

Based on the TV series *The Wild Thornberrys*® created by Klasky Csupo, Inc.
as seen on Nickelodeon®

SIMON SPOTLIGHT
An imprint of Simon & Schuster Children's Publishing Division
1230 Avenue of the Americas
New York, New York 10020

Manufactured in the United States of America

First Edition
2 4 6 8 10 9 7 5 3 1

ISBN 0-689-83430-6

Library of Congress Control Number 00-032235

Discovery Facts

Bora Bora: Located in the southern part of the Pacific Ocean, Bora Bora is known as one of the Society Islands. It is also considered by many to be the most beautiful of the Tahitian islands. Bora Bora is surrounded by a stunning lagoon.

Mount Pahia: A double-peaked mountain on Bora Bora, Mount Pahia is 2,030 feet high. It offers a view of the lagoon from the top.

Sea Turtles: These large turtles live in the ocean. There are at least seven different types of sea turtles, ranging in size from 100 to 1,500 pounds. Sea turtles have big heads, which they can't pull into their shells like other turtles.

Manta Rays: These flat-bodied sea creatures can grow up to twenty-two feet wide. They have "wings" which they use to swim. Manta rays are related to sharks. They are also called devilfish and devil rays.

Eliza Thornberry opened the door of the Commvee and looked out. It was a beautiful sunny day. She had big plans.

"Today is the day I go on an underwater walk in the lagoon!" she said to Darwin. "Are you sure you don't want to come?"

"Quite sure," replied Darwin.

"You get to go to this beautiful reef and see all these amazing tropical fish and sea horses and those huge manta rays and maybe even some sharks . . ."

"No thanks," replied Darwin. Sharks! That sounded too dangerous for him!

Eliza poured herself a bowl of cereal. It seemed very quiet. "Where are Mom and Dad?" she wondered aloud. Just then she noticed a note on the table. It said:

Good morning, girls!

What a beautiful day! Your father and I are hiking to the top of Mount Pahia to do some filming.

Will one of you please keep a close eye on Donnie today? And don't forget to meet us back at the Commvee at 1:00 on the dot. We have a surprise for you all!

Don't be late!

Love, Mom

Just then, Debbie walked outside.

"Where are you going?" Eliza asked.

"To the beach," said Debbie, putting on her sunglasses.

"Wait!" said Eliza. "I have plans today and someone has to keep an eye on Donnie."

Debbie laughed. "Hello! Earth to Eliza! How can I sunbathe *and* watch the wild boy?"

"But it's your turn to watch Donnie!" Eliza said. "I did it the last five times Mom asked!"

Debbie shrugged and took off for the beach.

Eliza sighed. She usually didn't mind watching Donnie at all. But kids under seven weren't allowed to walk on the lagoon floor. If she had to watch Donnie she wouldn't be able to go!

"This is so unfair!" Eliza said to Darwin. "Debbie is always telling me what to do. It's always 'Do the dishes, Eliza!' or 'Take out the garbage, Eliza!' or 'Scoop that scorpion out of the toilet, Eliza!'" She crossed her arms over her chest. "Well, I've had enough of being told what to do!"

"Eliza," interrupted Darwin, "where did Donnie go?"

The door to the Commvee was wide open. Eliza ran inside. But Donnie was gone.

"Oh, no!" she cried. "We'd better go find him!"

13

"I bet he went to the mango grove," said
Eliza. "Donnie loves mangoes."

They searched and searched, but Donnie
was nowhere to be found.

"Maybe he went to the forest," said Darwin. "You know how much he loves swinging from vines."

The two hiked to the middle of the island. The forest was dark and a little spooky.

"Donnie! Donnie, where are you?" they called.

But Donnie was nowhere to be found.

Back at the Commvee, they could hear someone moving around inside.

"Donnie?" Eliza said hopefully. She found herself face to face with Debbie instead.

"What's going on?" asked Debbie, who had just come back from the beach. "Where's Donnie?"

Eliza didn't say anything.

"You lost Donnie?" asked Debbie. "Boy, are you going to be in trouble!"

"Me?" shouted Eliza. "Why me?"

Darwin covered his eyes. He hated it when the two girls fought!

"You make me do everything!" said Eliza. "You think just because you're older, you can boss me around."

Debbie tossed her hair. "When you were little I always had to watch you. Well, now it's your turn!"

The two sisters frowned at each other.

Finally Eliza broke the silence. "I think I know where Donnie went. I bet he heard me talking about the lagoon."

The girls and Darwin ran to the lagoon as fast as they could.

"Now what?" asked Debbie.

"You and Darwin take that end," said Eliza, "and I'll take this end." They split up and started searching.

"Donnie, where are you?" called Eliza.

"Are you looking for someone?" asked a voice.

"Yes, I am," said Eliza. She turned around—but no one was there.

"Down here," said the voice.

Eliza looked down—and saw a huge sea turtle.

"Have you seen a little wild boy?" she asked.

"I am ninety-five years old and I have seen many things. I have seen a monsoon that made the palm trees bend over backward. I have seen boats that move without oars and flying machines that land on the water with people inside. Why I have even seen—"

"But have you seen a little wild boy?" Eliza interrupted.

"Why, yes, I have," replied the turtle. "He was heading toward the reef in an inner tube."

Eliza cupped her hand above her eyes and squinted. She could see something way out in the distance. Was it Donnie?

"I can help you find him," said the turtle.
"There's a boat on the beach. You can follow me."

"Okay," said Eliza. They had to find
Donnie—and soon!

Eliza ran down the beach to tell the others
her plan.

"Look, geek," Debbie said, "there's no way I'm
going out in the middle of the ocean
just because you have a
hunch Donnie is there.
That's crazy!"

Eliza looked Debbie straight in the eye. "You've got to trust me on this one," she said.

Debbie stared at her. "Oh, all right," she said. "But don't forget we're supposed to meet Mom and Dad back at the Commvee at one o'clock on the dot!"

The girls took turns paddling. After a while, they reached the reef. And there was Donnie, sitting on a big rock. He pointed at the water. Two huge manta rays were circling the rock he sat on.

"What's that?" said Debbie, leaning forward. Just then, one of the manta rays jumped into the air.

Eliza thought it looked very graceful. But Debbie was scared. She stood up—and knocked the boat over!

Luckily, they were all strong swimmers. In no time, they were all sitting on Donnie's rock. It was pretty crowded.

The boat started drifting away. "What are we going to do?" wailed Debbie. "I'm not going into that water with those horrible things!"

Eliza smiled. "Those are manta rays, Debbie," she explained to her sister. "They may be big and scary looking, but they're not dangerous at all." Eliza handed her glasses to Darwin and dove into the water.

Meanwhile, Nigel and Marianne were high atop Mount Pahia. They were admiring the beautiful colors of the lagoon. "I see something out there!" said Nigel, looking through his binoculars. "Could it be Eliza, Debbie, Darwin, and Donnie on a rock in the middle of the ocean?"

"Don't be silly, dear," said Marianne.

The reef was amazing! The turtle took Eliza for a quick tour. She swam among schools of colorful fish. Seahorses darted in and out of the coral. Then one of the manta rays swam up to her. She reached out and touched it. It was so soft!

With the turtle's help, Eliza brought the boat over to the rock. Everyone climbed in and they headed back to the beach.

"Wow, you were so brave!" said Debbie. She frowned. "I'm sorry you didn't get to go on your lagoon walk," she said. "The next time you want to do something dorky like that, *I'll* watch Donnie."

"Um, thanks," said Eliza. "I'll remind you next time. . . ."

"Time!" Debbie shouted. She looked down at her watch. "Oh, gosh, we've got to go meet Mom and Dad! Hurry!"

Luckily, the turtle knew a shortcut back to the Commvee. They were there in no time.

The big surprise was a picnic on a private island! Marianne smiled at the girls. "I just wanted to thank you for taking such good care of Donnie today," she said. "I'm sure if he knew the words, he'd thank you too!"

Just then Donnie reached over—and licked Eliza's face!

"Um, you're welcome!" said Eliza.